Go to the back of the book for your thrilling snakes and ladders board game!

Captain Flinn
and the
Pirate Dinosaurs

Missing Treasure!

Written by

Giles Andreae

Illustrated by

Russell Ayto

PUFFIN

For Ned – G.A.
For my mother and
father – R.A.

A note from the author:

"By the way, there is a dinosaur in this book called the **giganotosaurus.**
It's a hard word, so it might be a good idea if you learn how to say it now.
Take it bit by bit . . .

gig – an – OH – toe – SORE – us.

That's it!

Giganotosaurus!"

PUFFIN BOOKS
Published by the Penguin Group: London, New York, Australia, Canada,
India, Ireland, New Zealand and South Africa
Penguin Books Ltd,
Registered Offices: 80 Strand, London WC2R 0RL, England
puffinbooks.com
First published 2007
10 9 8 7 6 5 4 3 2 1
Text copyright © Giles Andreae, 2007
Illustrations copyright © Russell Ayto, 2007
All rights reserved
The moral right of the author and illustrator has been asserted
Printed in China
ISBN: 978-0-141-38206-7

Flinn's board – KEEP OFF!

This is Flinn. Flinn LOVES dinosaurs.

Tomorrow is a very special day because Flinn's teacher, Miss Pie, is taking his class to see the dinosaur skeletons at the museum.

"Here we are!"
said Miss Pie.
"Now remember –
stay together and

don't

touch

anything!"

Flinn's class followed
the museum guide to
the Skeleton Room.

"**Wow!**" said Flinn to his
friends, Pearl, Tom and Violet.
"That one looks really *scary*."

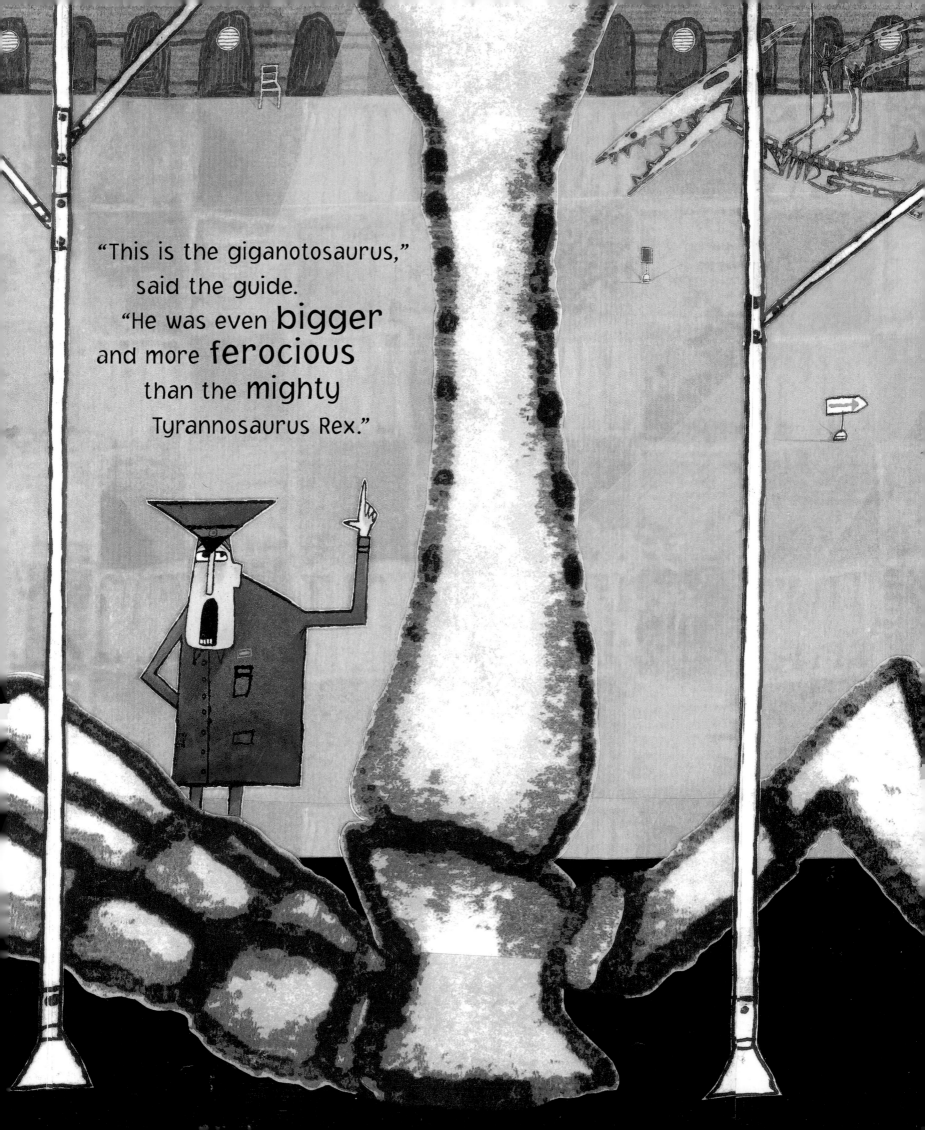

"This is the giganotosaurus,"
said the guide.
"He was even **bigger**
and more **ferocious**
than the **mighty**
Tyrannosaurus Rex."

In the next room, there was a big glass case.
But it was completely EMPTY!

"It used to hold the
treasure of the famous pirate
Captain Rufus Rumblebelly,"
explained the guide,
"but it was **stolen** last night!"

"Real pirate treasure?" said Flinn (who liked pirates
just as much as dinosaurs). "But **who** could have stolen it?"

"Look!" said Tom.
"Maybe these
peculiar feathers
are a clue . . ."

"They seem to be leading to that cupboard," said Pearl.

"Let's follow them!" said Violet.

So Flinn and his friends quietly opened the door and slipped through.

The cupboard was cold
and dark and full of
cobwebs.

"Wait a minute!"
said Flinn. "What's that?"

He bent down
and picked up a
gleaming golden coin.

"And look!
Here's another one."

"It must be the treasure!"
said Violet.

And just at that moment,
the back of the cupboard fell away
and Flinn and his friends
all
tumbled
out . . .

"What treasure?" asked Flinn,
as he quickly untied the pirate.

"Why, the famous treasure of
Rufus Rumblebelly!" said the pirate.
"I'm Gordon Gurgleguts and Rufus
Rumblebelly was my granddaddy.
I took the treasure from the museum –
just to have a little look – but then
someone stole it from **me**!!"

"That's **amazing!**" said Flinn.
"We're looking for the treasure too!
We'll help you find it,
but **only if** you promise
to take it **straight**
back to the museum."

"All right," said Gurgleguts.
"I promise."

"But who stole it?"
    asked Flinn.
"I don't know," said Gurgleguts.
    "But I did hear a strange song as they sailed away.
    It went:

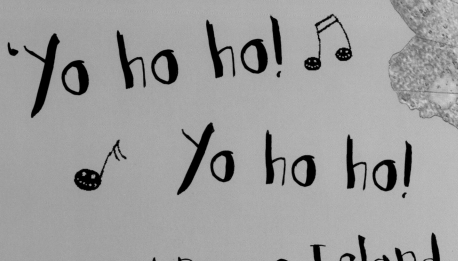

'Yo ho ho!
Yo ho ho!
Bag o' Bones Island
Here we go!'"

"Then that's where **we'll** go!"
said Flinn. "To Bag o' Bones
Island! Come on, everyone!"
    "Aye, aye!" said Gurgleguts.
"And why don't YOU be our captain?
Here – take my hat."

So Captain Flinn took the helm and they swiftly
set sail for Bag o' Bones Island.

"Island ahoy!" shouted
Pirate Violet from the crow's nest.

"Follow me, everyone,"
said Captain Flinn.
"There's thick jungle
ahead and we don't
want anyone to get lost . . ."

"Gurgleguts? Gurgleguts?"

"WHERE ARE YOU?"

"Wait," said Pirate Pearl.
"What's that noise?"

In front of them was a clearing. Captain Flinn peered into it and shuddered.
"Pirates!" he said. "But they're not just ordinary pirates. They're . . .

"...PIRATE DINOSAURS!"
And he was right!
There was . . .

A PIRATE DIPLODOCUS . . .

A PIRATE STEGOSAURUS . . .

A PIRATE TRICERATOPS . . .

AND A GREAT BIG PIRATE TYRANNOSAURUS REX.

Beside the Pirate Dinosaurs was a huge pile of gleaming treasure. And next to the treasure, tied up from head to foot, was GURGLEGUTS.

The Pirate Dinosaurs were singing a terrible song:

"We've stolen all the treasure
We'll use it at our leisure
And won't it be a pleasure
For us all to live like kings!

And don't think we've forgotten
That this pirate's rather rotten
So let's barbecue his bottom
With some spicy chicken wings!"

"Stop!" yelled Captain Flinn.
"Untie my friend **immediately!**"

"We couldn't possibly do that,"
said the Tyrannosaurus Rex,
squeezing a huge dollop of
tomato ketchup on to Gurgleguts' head.
"Because we're going to

EAT HIM UP!"

"Well then, you slimy seafaring sausages,"
said Captain Flinn, drawing his cutlass,
"you nasty *noodle-brained* nincompoops,
you dirty *dastardly* dunderheads—
you're going to have to

eat

me

first!

ATTACK!"

CRASH!

Suddenly, Captain Flinn took a huge **swipe** at the Tyrannosaurus Rex, and **pinned** him up against a tree.
"Please spare me,"
said the Tyrannosaurus Rex,
"and I promise to be
the goodest goody in the
whole world . . . EVER."

"You great **big fibber!**" said Captain Flinn.
"Fibber, eh?" said the Tyrannosaurus Rex angrily.
"Well then, I think it's time you met my cousin!"

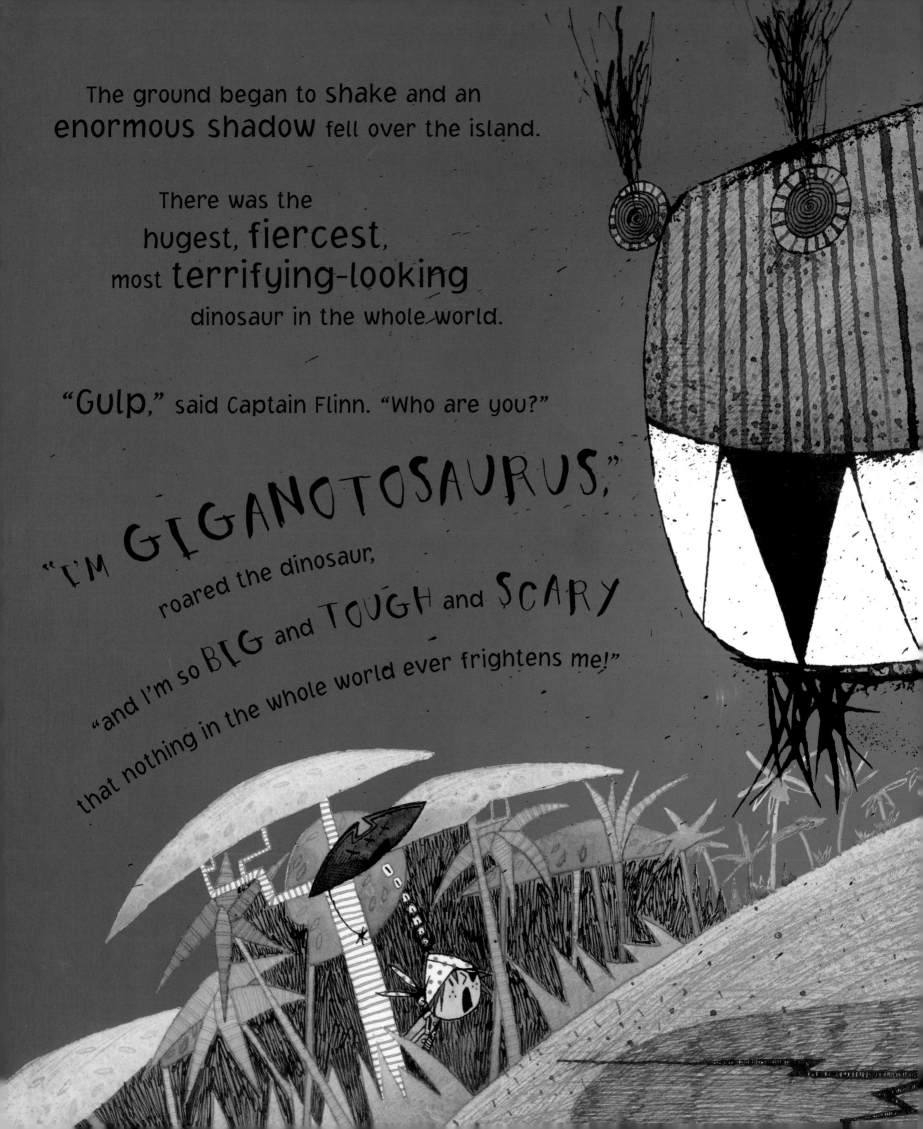

The ground began to shake and an **enormous shadow** fell over the island.

There was the
hugest, fiercest,
most terrifying-looking
dinosaur in the whole world.

"Gulp," said Captain Flinn. "Who are you?"

"I'm GIGANOTOSAURUS,"
roared the dinosaur,
"and I'm so BIG and TOUGH and SCARY
that nothing in the whole world ever frightens me!"

Then suddenly . . .

"HHH!"

cried the Giganotosaurus.

"Spider! Spider!
Help! HEEEELP!!"

A tiny spider was hanging
from Captain Flinn's
pirate hat.

"Well, shiver me timbers," said Flinn.
"Fancy a big old dinosaur being
scared of a teeny-weeny spider!"

"They're just so creepy and crawly,"
wailed the Giganotosaurus.
"Keep him away
from me – please!"

In all the commotion,
Captain Flinn saw his chance.

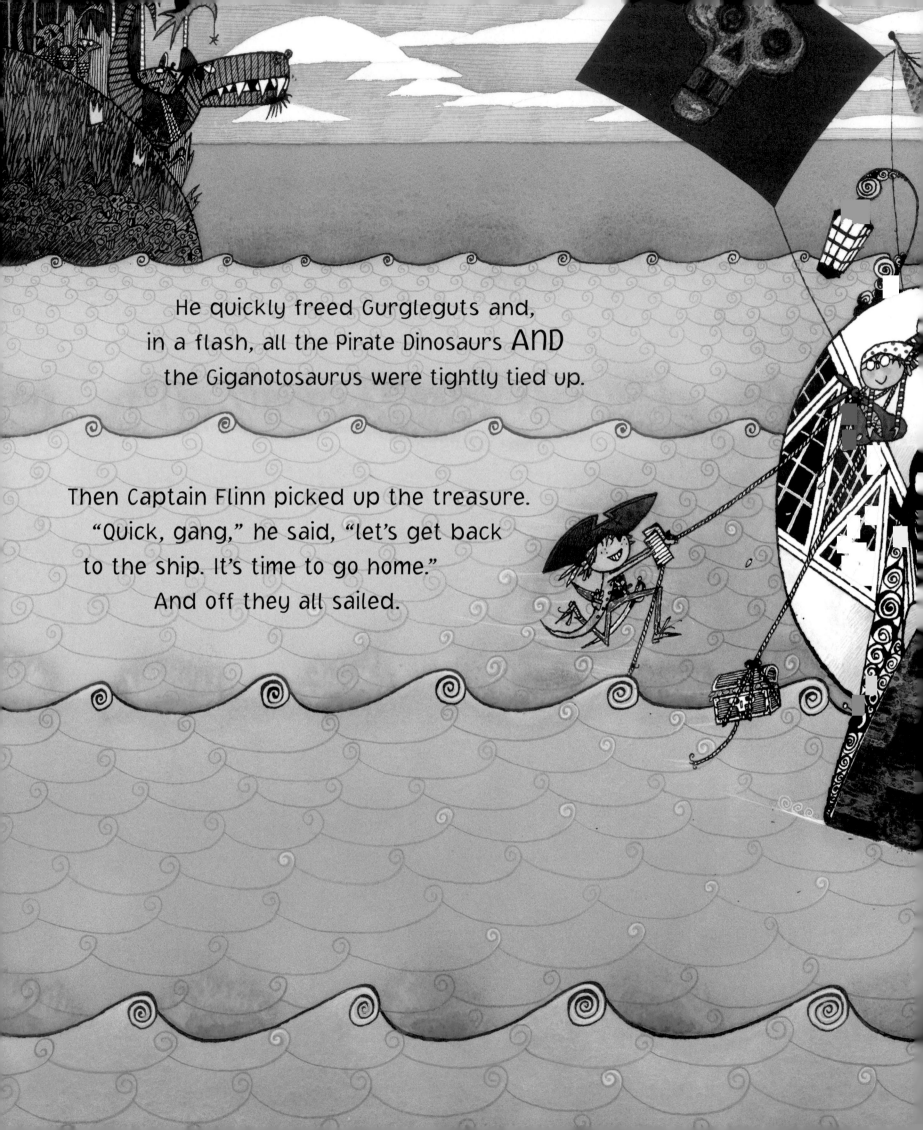

He quickly freed Gurgleguts and,
in a flash, all the Pirate Dinosaurs AND
the Giganotosaurus were tightly tied up.

Then Captain Flinn picked up the treasure.
"Quick, gang," he said, "let's get back
to the ship. It's time to go home."
And off they all sailed.

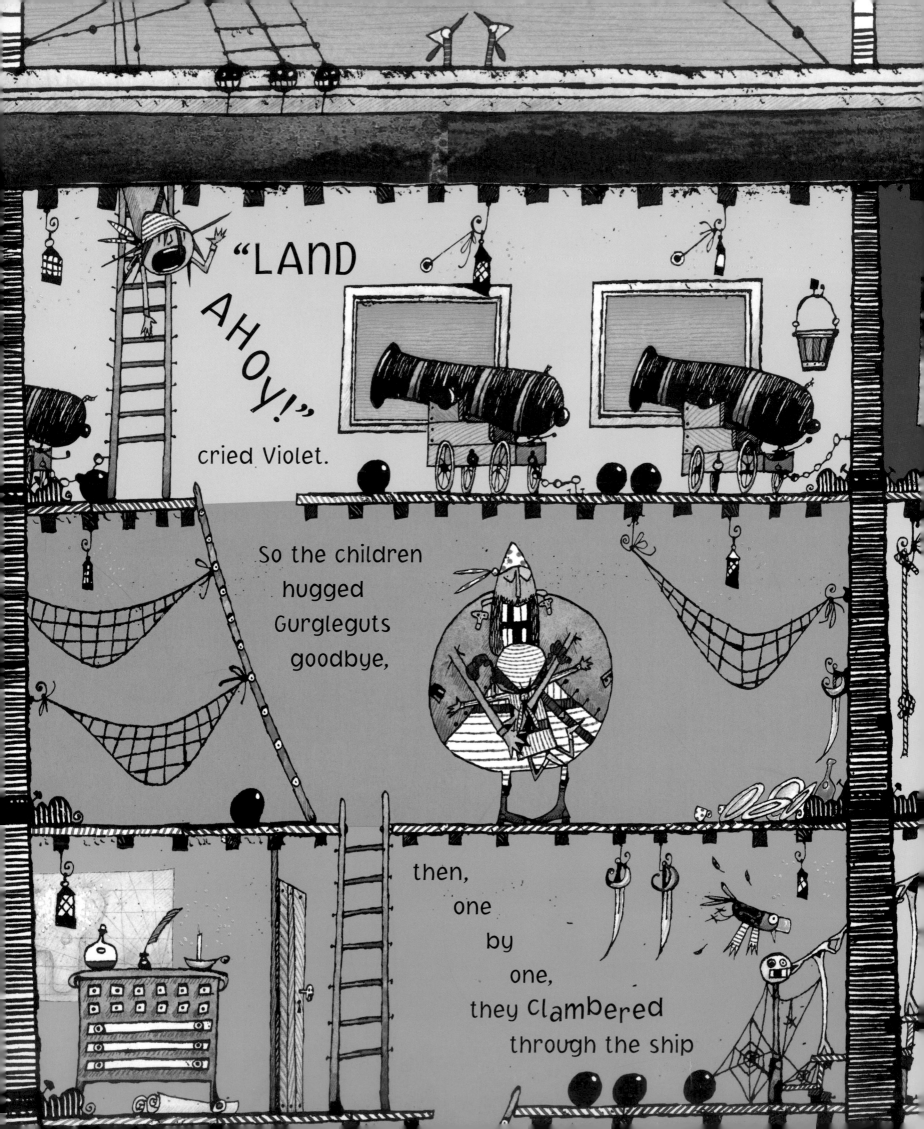

"LAND AHOY!" cried Violet.

So the children hugged Gurgleguts goodbye, then, one by one, they clambered through the ship

into the open cupboard . . . .

. . . and back
into the museum.
"Wherever have you been?"
said Miss Pie.
"We've found the missing
treasure!" said Flinn.
"My goodness!" said the
museum guide. "Well done!
But WHO stole it?"

"It's a long story," said Flinn. "But it ended up in the hands of some pirates. Oh, and they weren't just pirates, they were PIRATE DINOSAURS!"

"Pirate Dinosaurs!" laughed the guide. "That's the silliest thing I've heard in my whole life! Pirate Dinosaurs indeed!"

"And just for your information," added Flinn, "I can tell you something about your giganotosaurus. He was **frightened** of **spiders**. Very **frightened indeed.**"

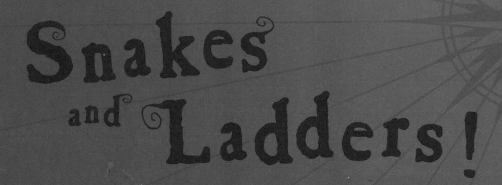

Snakes and Ladders!

Heave-ho, me hearties! Are YOU brave enough to face the dangers of the deep?

You will need

- A dice
- Pieces of eight – plunder your money box for coins to use as counters!
- 2–4 pirates

How to play

Put on your pirate hat and decide who is going to go first. Roll the dice and move your coin the number of spaces shown.

If you land on the bottom of some rigging, climb all the way to the top. GO-AAAR-R-GGGGH!

But if you land on a sea serpent's head, slide all the way down to its tail. SEAFARING SAUSAGES, IT'S TIME TO WALK THE PLANK!

The first pirate to reach the treasure is the winner!